# PATTERNS IN PERU

## AN ADVENTURE IN PATTERNING

CINDY NEUSCHWANDER

ILLUSTRATED BY BRYAN LANGDO



Henry Holt and Company

New York

*For Tim—*

*Strong work!*

*—C. N.*

*For Nikki, and our adventure together*

*—B. L.*

Henry Holt and Company, LLC
*Publishers since 1866*
175 Fifth Avenue
New York, New York 10010
www.henryholtchildrensbooks.com


Distributed in Canada by H. B. Fenn and Company Ltd.

Library of Congress Cataloging-in-Publication Data
Neuschwander, Cindy.
Patterns in Peru : an adventure in patterning / Cindy Neuschwander; illustrated by Bryan Langdo.—1st ed.
p. cm.
ISBN-13: 978-0-8050-7954-8 / ISBN-10: 0-8050-7954-8
1. Pattern perception—Juvenile literature. 2. Sequences (Mathematics)—Juvenile literature. I. Langdo, Bryan, ill. II. Title.
Q327.N48 2007 152.14'23—dc22 2006002871

First Edition—2007 / Designed by Amy Manzo Toth
The artist used Winsor & Newton watercolors on Fabriano Artistic paper to create the illustrations for this book.
Printed in the United States of America on acid-free paper. ∞

1 3 5 7 9 10 8 6 4 2

"Matt," said his twin sister, Bibi, "did you have to wear that shirt to the museum? All those stripes are making me dizzy!"

Matt smiled. "I think I look very South American," he said.

The Zills family was in Peru. Matt and Bibi's parents were scientists who had come to help Professor Oswaldo Herrera inspect an ancient weaving at the Incan Museum.

"This is a man's tunic," said their father, Dr. William Zills. "It's at least five hundred years old."

"And it's finely woven, with lots of unusual patterns," added their mother, Dr. Jillian Zills. "It probably belonged to someone special."

Professor Herrera nodded eagerly. "I think this tunic belonged to the secret messenger for the Lost City of Quwi [pronounced COO-ee]. It was a hidden city known only to the emperor, his court, and this messenger. Many people have searched for Quwi but no one has ever found it."

"Maybe we can," said the twins.

"Arrowff!" added their dog, Riley.

"We can look for it, but we'll have to travel on foot," said Professor Herrera. "You two can ride on guanacos. They're cousins of the llama."

When Matt climbed onto his guanaco, he grinned at his sister. "**GUA**-naco for a ride?"

"It's pronounced gua-**NA**-co," corrected Bibi. As she said this, both animals galloped off, leaving everyone but Riley far behind. They ended up on a highland plateau framed by towering mountains.

"Brrr! It's cold." Bibi shivered. She opened her satchel and took out a poncho. Matt peered into his pack.

"Hey, Bibi!" he exclaimed. "This is the tunic that Mom and Dad looked at. It must have been put in here by mistake." Matt was so cold he put it on.

"Do I look like an ancient Incan?" he asked. He slapped his hands and stamped his feet to stay warm. *Clap-clap-stomp-stomp . . . clap-clap-stomp-stomp.*

"Matt!" said Bibi excitedly. "That clapping reminds me of something. Mom said this tunic had very unusual patterns. Maybe the *patterns* are the secret to finding the Lost City. You could be wearing the messenger's *map*!"

"Then point me in the right direction," he said.

"Well," Bibi said, "this first pattern shows llamas and plateaus. That's where we are now. The next one is a repeating pattern. It goes up and down like mountains. But what about these dots?"

On the lines slanting up, there were four dots. On the lines slanting down, there were two.

Matt ignored his sister's question and rode up the mountain trail. Bibi and Riley followed. They reached the top and started going down the other side.

Bibi looked down the steep mountainside. "This path is really narrow!"

"Don't worry!" said Matt, turning around. "We'll be . . . WHAAHHH!"

He tumbled off his guanaco and over the edge of the trail. He grabbed a nearby tree root and held on. But part of the tunic tore and fluttered away.

"Matt! Are you okay?"

"I . . . I . . . I guess so," he stammered, climbing back onto the path. "We'd better walk down this part."

"That was a close call!" said Bibi. She looked at the tunic. "I think the dots are a travel warning."

Matt looked confused.

"Use four guanaco feet when going up but use your own two feet when going down," Bibi explained.

"Patterns can be complicated!" said Matt.

"But they never fail," said Bibi. "You just have to figure them out."

The twins rode up and walked down two more short, steep mountain passes.

They stopped at the edge of a cliff. A flimsy rope bridge swayed before them. A river roared below.

"It's not very far across," encouraged Bibi.

"Yeah, but it's a *looong* way down," Matt said nervously.

"The pattern tells us where to walk." Bibi pointed to the tunic. "See how every third line is X-ed out? Just step over those ropes." The twins started to cross.

"On . . . on . . . over. On . . . on . . . over," repeated Matt.

"Don't look down!" warned Bibi.

Just then Riley stepped onto an X-ed out rope. "AHROOOO!" he howled as his front legs plunged through the unraveling braids.

"I'm definitely following this pattern," Matt said, yanking Riley up.

Safe on the other side, the three explorers hiked a short distance into the jungle. Colorful parrots squawked at them.

"Look at the patterns on those birds!" said Matt. He was starting to see patterns everywhere.

A thick wall of vines hung before them. The twins were unsure where to go next.

At that moment, Riley noticed something small and furry. Matt saw it, too.

"Awww!" he said. "It's a guinea pig!" The tiny creature squeaked and dove under some leaves. They chased after it.

BUMP! They ran into something behind the vines. Pulling away the plants, Matt came face-to-face with a large stone carving on a wall.

"Wow!" he said. "It's Super Inca Man!"

"It's the symbol for Incan royalty!" cried Bibi excitedly. She remembered seeing a statue like it in the Incan Museum. "This must be the Lost City!"

"Where's the entrance?" asked Matt. He started to climb the wall, but when he put his foot on the carving, it began to turn.

"Yikes!" he yelled, jumping down.

"That explains this guy on the tunic doing cartwheels!" said Bibi.

"What kind of pattern is that?" wondered Matt.

"It's one where a single picture turns around in a special order," answered his sister.

"Like a giant combination lock?" asked Matt.

"Exactly!" replied Bibi.

The twins carefully turned the figure just as the tunic showed and a heavy stone door slowly opened.

"Are we inside the Lost City?" asked Matt.

"Not yet," answered Bibi. They faced another high wall. It was covered with panels of animal carvings.

"It reminds me of the last pattern on the tunic!" said Bibi. "There were nine squares and each one had different animals in it."

But some of it had been torn away when Matt fell. He hung his head. "I'm sorry it ripped," he said.

"Don't worry," said Bibi. "Patterns are predictable. If we can figure out this first part, we can figure out the rest."

"These foxes are cool," said Matt, tapping one of the pictures.

WHUMP! A grass net closed quickly around Riley and lifted him into the air.

"Careful, Matt!" warned Bibi as she untangled Riley. "This place is booby-trapped! Only touch the correct square."

"Which square *is* the right one?" he asked. "I don't see any pattern."

Bibi was busy counting the animals in the first squares: three foxes, six llamas, nine parrots.

"It's a growing pattern!" Bibi said. "Each square adds three more animals!" She drew a t-chart in the dirt. "The ninth square should have twenty-seven!"

They started counting the animals in each panel.

"There!" shouted Matt. "Twenty-seven guinea pigs are in that square!" He carefully touched the stone. It slid open!

From inside, the twins could hear a faint sound. "*Quwi . . . quwi . . . quwi.*"

"That sounds like someone announcing the name of the city," said Bibi.

They all climbed through. The view on the other side was breathtaking! The ruins of an entire city lay complete and undisturbed.

Matt bent down and picked up a small striped creature. "Even the guinea pigs here have patterns!" he said.

"*Quwi!*" it squeaked.

# A NOTE TO TEACHERS AND PARENTS

Recognizing, describing, and extending patterns are important pre-algebra skills for young children to develop. *Patterns in Peru* introduces three types of patterns: repeating, positional, and growing. Here are some activities you can try for more fun with patterns:

- Encourage children to recognize patterns wherever they are. When they see a pattern, let them describe it to you.
- Clapping and stomping, as Matt did in the story, is a good way of practicing aural, or sound, sequences. You and a child can make up fun clapping patterns for others to copy.
- Have children make pictures of shirts with colorful repeating patterns. Then they can add drawings of their own faces to make self-portraits with patterns.
- Ask children to describe patterns using letters instead of words. The "on, on, over" pattern in the story could be described as A, A, B. This teaches children to use variables, an important pre-algebra skill.
- Make a copy of the emperor's symbol from the story. Ask children to turn the figure to re-create the positional pattern on the tunic, just as Matt and Bibi did.
- Make a set of cards that skip count by any certain number. After seeing a few cards, ask children to predict what number will come next. This gives them practice in finding unknowns.
- Have children try skip counting by 10 but begin with a number like 7. If they can count 7, 17, 27, etc., you can be sure they understand a "plus ten" pattern. Try variations of this activity, skip counting by other numbers.
- In the story, Bibi makes a t-chart to help her predict the ninth position in a growing pattern. Create some t-charts with your child. If one guanaco has four legs and two guanacos have eight legs, how many legs do ten guanacos have? In this way, children can begin to work with mathematical functions.

*Whatever activities you try, you can help children enjoy the math!*